Sir Gawain,
feeling rather green,

Sir Ack,
who's fond of eating lots,

Sir Mordred,
hatching horrid plots.

Morgana,
Arthur's wicked
sister,

Merlin.
That's me,
your wizard mister!

To
Megan Larkin, Sarah Dudman & Ruth Alltimes,
my edifying editors at the Court of Camelot.
With bows and courtesies, Tony Mitton.

ORCHARD BOOKS
96 Leonard Street, London EC2A 4XD
Orchard Books Australia
32/45-51 Huntley Street, Alexandria, NSW 2015
First published in Great Britain in 2004
First paperback edition 2005
Text © Tony Mitton 2004
Illustrations © Arthur Robins 2004
The rights of Tony Mitton to be identified as the author
and Arthur Robins as the illustrator of this work
have been asserted by them in accordance with the
Copyright, Designs, and Patents Act, 1988.
A CIP catalogue record for this book is available
from the British Library.
ISBN 1 84362 000 6 (hardback)
ISBN 1 84362 004 9 (paperback)
1 3 5 7 9 10 8 6 4 2 (hardback)
1 3 5 7 9 10 8 6 4 2 (paperback)
Printed in Great Britain

In the days of good King Arthur
when men wore suits of armour,
a normal knight was good and right
as well as a real charmer.

But although King Arthur's followers
so fairly ruled the land,
there were one or two among his crew
who secretly schemed and planned.

At good old-fashioned chivalry
King Arthur's court was best.
But you always get some dodgy guy
who spoils it for the rest.

I am the wizard Merlin,
and in my head I hold
the tales of Crazy Camelot,
just waiting to be told.

Now give me just a moment
to drink my cup of tea.
Then let me read the tea leaves
to see which it will be.

Ah, this one tells how Arthur
got diddled good and proper.
That mighty king lost everything
and really came a cropper!

King Arthur's evil sister,
the witch Morgana la Fay,
was working at her magic
to blow the King away.

Her moody son, called Mordred,
who was one of Arthur's knights,
said,

Soon I'll own *my* uncle's throne,
with *my* name above in lights.

Morgana had tried to steal the crown,
but Arthur had always won.
"Well, if it can't be mine," she crooned,
"I'll snatch it for my son."

She schemed away with Mordred.
They made a deadly pair.
Whenever they got together
a chill passed through the air.

Now the Danes were threatening Britain.
They were planning raids from France.
So Mordred said to Morgana,

Right, Mum. Here comes our chance.

He went to see King Arthur
and offered his support.
"While you're away I'll gladly stay
and rule for you at court."

Somebody has to be at home
and miss out on the fun.
Besides, I think I've sprained my wrist,
so I should be the one.

Arthur was very grateful.
"Yes…we need a minder here.
Make sure the daily dusting's done.
And don't drink all the beer."

Look after my wife Guinevere.
Make sure the staff behave.
Keep everything in order
while we're off being brave.

He summoned up his forces,
then rode off to the war,
not realising that Mordred
was rotten to the core.

As soon as all the royal ships
were safely off at sea,
sly Mordred and Morgana
both danced about with glee.

They captured poor Queen Guinevere
and locked her in a tower.
And then Morgana cast a spell
to seize the royal power.

She waved her witchy hands around.
The breeze began to sing.
And soon the whole of Camelot
thought Mordred was the king.

Except for good old Merlin
who hid out in the wood.
"I'll wait till Arthur's back," he said,
"then try to do some good.

Morgana with son Mordred
set up a second spell
to make quite sure their wicked plot
would all run smooth and well.

It meant that if King Arthur
got wounds, however slight,
he'd grow so weak and feeble
he'd lose at any fight.

Morgana spelled as Mordred stirred
and this is what she said,

The smallest battle wound he gets will drain him till he's dead.

Abroad, the royal forces
had squashed the Danish foe.
They all came gladly sailing home,
but then they gulped,

For there upon the beach they saw
the sad and ugly sight
of Mordred and their countrymen
preparing for a fight.

"This is Morgana's doing,"
growled Arthur. "I've been had.
Why did I trust you, Mordred?
You naughty boy, you're bad."

"I'm not just bad," leered Mordred.
"I'm wicked and I'm shrewd.
I've made the throne on loan my own.
Ha ha! I'm topmost dude!

"But fight me for it, if you like.
I'm bound to be the winner."
"I'll have your head," King Arthur said,

to feed my dogs for dinner.

Then through the air came Merlin
upon a silvery cloud.
"Hey! Knock it off!" he called to them.

This battle's not allowed.

He waved a wand to stop the fight
and pause the wicked plan,
persuading Mordred and the King
to meet up man to man.

"But while you talk," warned Merlin,
"let no one show their blade.
For that would send a signal
that battle's to be made."

So both the armies sheathed their swords
while Mordred and the King
sat down to make a treaty
and sort out everything.

But while the armies waited,
a snake came sliding out.
It slithered up towards a knight
and reared its ugly snout!

"A serpent!" gasped the startled man.
"It's poisonous! Take care!"
He quickly drew his shining sword
and waved it in the air.

The serpent ducked the deadly blade
and swiftly turned around.
It found its hole in seconds flat
and bolted underground.

It must have been Morgana
in deadly snake disguise.
Its horrid hiss was just like hers –
and did you see those eyes!?

Now, as the brave knight swirled
    his sword,
it sparkled in the sun.
His weapon waving in the air
was seen by everyone.

"A blade is drawn. The battle's on!"
The cry was passed about.
And soon each knight joined in the fight
with clash and clank and shout.

The swords and clubs went whirling.
Tough shields were sliced in two.
Some knights sat down exhausted
and some cried, "Boo-hoo-hoo!"

Mordred duelled with Arthur.
He nicked him on the finger.
And once he'd got that cut in
he had no need to linger.

But no one won the battle.
It just destroyed the army.
"This plan was really silly,"
moaned Mordred. "I've been barmy!

"I've gone and made a mess of things.
I wish Mum hadn't helped.
It looks like Camelot is doomed.
I'm off!" the villain yelped.

"Oh, darn it!" cursed Morgana.
"Another messed-up plot."
She packed her black bikini
and flew off somewhere hot.

Though Merlin tried to melt the spell,
Morgana's power was stronger.
Arthur had a finger-graze
and wouldn't last much longer.

A tiny little cut like that
ought not to be so tragic.
But that's the kind of thing that happens
when you mess with magic.

So Merlin patched the finger up
with sparkly sticking plaster.
"And now the sword must be returned,"
he murmured to his master.

"I'm much too weak for that!"
    wailed Arthur.

Though I know I should.
That lake is hidden miles away
beyond the magic wood.

"I'll take you," said Sir Bedevere,
upon his bended knee.
"I'll lead you gently on my horse.
Just come along with me."

So Bedevere took Arthur
and went to find the lake,
while Merlin vanished to his cave.
He'd magic still to make.

He had to sort things out a bit.
For, after Arthur's reign,
he knew there might be trouble
and we'd need him once again.

After a gruelling journey,
the King and Bedevere
lay panting by that silver lake
that lay so still and clear.

"And now," croaked poor King Arthur,
"I know it sounds bizarre.
But take my sword Excalibur
and chuck it way out far."

"A whizzo sword!?" shrieked Bedevere.
"What, bung the thing away!?"
"Oh, don't go on," groaned Arthur.
"Please do it like I say."

But Bedevere just hid the
and hurled a rock instead.
"I've done it now, your hig.
he murmured, blushing red.

"It landed in the middle
and sank without a trace."
"You fibber," gasped King Arthur.
"I see it in your face."

"... admit," said Bedevere,
"... ms a blooming shame.
... sword like that upon my hip
would really bring me fame."

But Bedevere picked up the sword
and hurled it through the air.
An arm came rising from the lake.
The King said,

See. Look there.

The strange hand caught and held
the sword,
then drew it down below.
Poor Bedevere just gawped at it
and faintly murmured,

Just then a silent boat drew up
with women dressed in white.
"We've come to take King Arthur.
His time has come. All right?"

So Bedevere helped Arthur in,
and gave a tearful wave.
The boat slid into eerie mists
to take him to his grave.

And no one knows quite where that is
but one thing's often said:
If ever we're in trouble
he'll come back from the dead.

He'll fetch his sword Excalibur
and say, "OK! Stay calm!"
Then ride out with his nutty knights
to save us all from harm.

And that's a magic prophecy.
I brewed it in my cup.
But now it's time to cut the rhyme
and wrap the series up.

So, this is Merlin kipping down.
I'm pretty tired as well.
If people ask you where I am,
I beg you! Please don't tell.

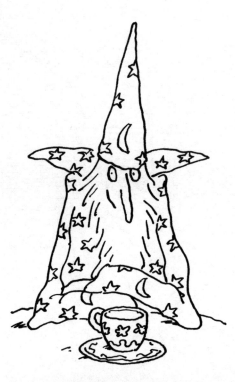

CRAZY CAMELOT CAPERS

Written by Tony Mitton
Illustrated by Arthur Robins

KING ARTHUR AND THE MIGHTY CONTEST
ISBN 1 84121 714 X   £3.99

EXCALIBUR THE MAGIC SWORD
ISBN 1 84121 718 2   £3.99

SIR LANCELOT AND THE BLACK KNIGHT
ISBN 1 84121 722 0   £3.99

SIR GAWAIN AND THE GREEN KNIGHT
ISBN 1 84121 726 3   £3.99

SIR GALAHAD AND THE GRAIL
ISBN 1 84362 001 4   £3.99

MORGANA THE SPOOKY SORCERESS
ISBN 1 84362 002 2   £3.99

BIG SIR B AND THE MONSTER MAID
ISBN 1 84362 003 0   £3.99

MEAN MORDRED AND THE FINAL BATTLE
ISBN 1 84362 004 9   £3.99

Crazy Camelot Capers are available from all good bookshops,
or can be ordered direct from the publisher:
Orchard Books, PO BOX 29, Douglas IM99 1BQ
Credit card orders please telephone 01624 836000
or fax 01624 837033
or e-mail: bookshop@enterprise.net for details.

To order please quote title, author and ISBN
and your full name and address.
Cheques and postal orders should be
made payable to 'Bookpost plc'.
Postage and packing is FREE within the UK
(overseas customers should add £1.00 per book).

Prices and availability are subject to change.

CRAZY CAMELOT

MEET THE KNIGHTS OF THE ROUND TABLE:

King Arthur
with his sword so bright,

Sir Percival,
a wily knight.

Sir Kay,
a chap whose hopes are high,

Sir Lancelot,
makes ladies sigh.

Mean Mordred

and the
Final Battle

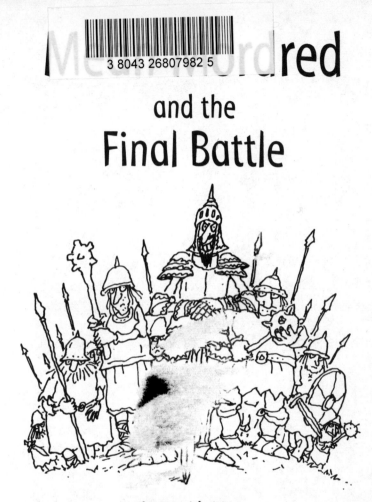

Tony Mitton
Illustrated by Arthur Robins

ORCHARD BOOKS